MW00901394

NOW WHAT?

words by **Brenda Faatz**
pictures by **Peter Trimarco**

notable kids publishing

"Imagination is what allows your mind to discover."
– Wassily Kandinsky (Russian Painter 1866-1944)

For our boys, Chandler Carter, Tad Trimarco and Jon Trimarco,
and to all our children at the Notable Kids Arts Center.

Library of Congress Control Number: 2021942127
Faatz, Brenda
Trimarco, Peter
Now What? / written by Brenda Faatz / Peter Trimarco and illustrated by Peter Trimarco – 1st ed.
Summary: Curiosity, frustration, anticipation, and an imaginative perspective are at the heart of this tale about Lizzy, the primary protagonist, and her new neighbor.
This book introduces Luna, who is from the Caribbean, as two children and their cultures come together to celebrate music, art, games and thinking outside the box on a day of unexpected adventures.

A free extensive curriculum is available to educators and librarians at www.notablekidspublishing.com/teacherguides

ISBN 9 7 8 1 7 3 3 3 5 4 8 2 0 [Juvenile Fiction – ages 4-8]

JUVENILE FICTION/ Social Themes/Emotions & Feelings. JUVENILE FICTION/ Imagination & Play

notablekids
publishing

Printed in the USA at Worzalla Printers
Notable Kids Publishing, Box 2047, Parker, Colorado 80134 / 303.840.5787 / www.notablekidspublishing.com
Typography: Museo 300. The illustrations were created with graphite, pastels and watercolor pencils on bristol board, with backgrounds painted in acrylic on canvas.
Spot colors and finish work created in photoshop. No kittens were harmed in the creation of this book of fiction.
Special thanks to Kay and Gordon LeBlanc Jr.

What does one do on a day such as this,
a little bit gray and a little bit "ish"?

Lizzy began with an indoor sport
of a bingity-boingity-bouncity sort.

"Uh-oh..."

"YIKES!"

"Now What?"

"Music, by gum!
I think I'll play some."

How about something
that's rockin' or jazzy?

...or snazzy pizazzy?

...or straight up *fantazzy?*

"Now What?"

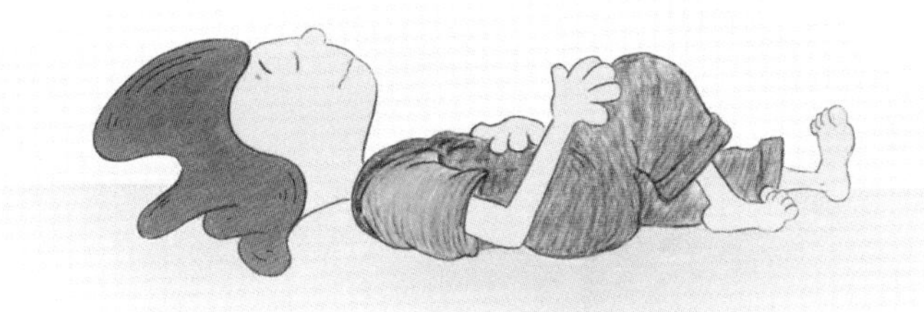

“Okay.”

Wet ball and all with a leap and a bound,
Lizzy went out with her light-hearted hound.

A throw and a catch and a hole in the ground
to bury a ball... but... "What is that sound?"

“It’s kittens! Small kittens! Cute kittens I see!
They’re only a dollar. They’re practically free!”

Kittens
$1 each

"It isn't so much that it's bad to have critters,
it just isn't wise if you get them in litters."

"Now what do I do with these sweet little kitties?
I must find a home for each of these pretties."

Lizzy opened for business with kittens to sell.
They were fluffy and free, so of course it went well.

But not far away there began some loud thumping
and clanking and clunking and bumping and whumping.

There were boxes stacked high and a bear on a chair.
"Good golly, wow-zolly! What's happening there?"

A little bit nervous with tummy a-flutter,
Lizzy peeked over some boxes and clutter.

"What do I see? Are you kidding me?
It's a person my size! What a happy surprise!"

"I'm Lizzy." "I'm Luna,"
each said with a smile.
"I like your sneakers." "And I like your style."

They talked and unpacked and began to discover
how different they were, yet the same as each other.

"I just love reading."
"I love to explore."
"I moved from an island."
"I walked from next door."

Then out of the boxes
flew treasures galore,
like chalk to draw hopscotch,
a game both adore.

There were costumes and bubbles and baubles and goggles
and spinning tops wobbling with jiggles and joggles.

"Now What?"
Lizzy asked, giddy with glee.

"Grandma's musical box!" Luna said.
"Come and see."

Out came maracas and two kinds of drums
and gourds that were made into two kinds of fun.

Shake-a-shake, rat-a-tat, clickity-clack,
in rhythm they jammed with a slap-a-tap-tap.

Now What?

The boxes! That's it!
The perfect space ship!

Using scissors and tape and the doggy's design,
one box at a time the ship started to climb.

With chalk, paint, and crayons they fancied it up...BUT...

NOW WHAT?

A runaway kitten ?!!!

aaaaaaaaaaaand....

...there goes the pup!

"Now What?!!"
"Now What?"

Clearly, their space-travel plans were cut short.
So, what was a rocket became a fine fort.

They giggled and gabbed as the rain tumbled down,
inside and cozy, enjoying the sound.
Luna told tales from the books she had read,
and Lizzy shared tunes she made up in her head.

Drippidy drizzle and plippedy plop,
the soppy rain finally came to a stop.

"It's blotchy and blurry
and smeary and smudgy."

"Our hopscotch is soup
and our fort is all sludgy."

"Now What!?!"

"Hold on!" Luna said.

"Lookie here!" Lizzy cried.
With wide-open wonder they saw with new eyes.

"If we add some dots here and a splotch of paint there,
paw prints make petals with freckle-dee flair!"

Chalk dust was billowing, pink-purple hues
with paint splashes dappling, green-yellow-blues.

They crafted their world with big, colorful choices,
expressing themselves in their own unique voices.

Then Lizzy and Luna sat back and reflected
on how their whole day was just so unexpected...
How thump-whumpy noises brought new friends together
and wet-wonky weather made things even better.

They walked and they talked as they painted and played,
with kitten and pup in their pint-size parade.
To answer "Now What?" was no longer their quest,
for to be in the moment was simply the best.